WILL YOU READ WITH ME?

YOU READ WITH ME?

WILL YOU READ WITH ME?

WILL YOU READ WITH ME?

Monkeys on a Fast

Text: Kaushik Viswanath
Illustrations: Shilpa Ranade
Typography: Soumitra Ranade
Design: Crimson

Karadi Tales Company Pvt. Ltd.
3A Dev Regency, 11 First Main Road,
Gandhinagar, Adyar,
Chennai 600 020.
Ph: +91 44 4205 4243
Email: contact@karaditales.com
Website: www.karaditales.com

First Reprint October 2009

Printed:

ISBN No. : 978-81-8190-156-9

MONKEYS ON A FAST

Kaushik Viswanath
Shilpa Ranade

What does this book do?

This series is a personal invitation to all children to read along with their favourite icons. Each narrator begins by asking, "Will you read with me?", and takes the child on a journey into the world of the story. In today's world, such a flight of fantasy is essential for the child's creative thought processes. Reading along with an audiobook offers the child an easy and non-threatening environment.

Each story has carefully been crafted to provoke the child's imagination; each illustration has been rendered with sensitivity to open up the imagination and set it free; music for each story has been composed to create a complete ambience for the story; most importantly, each narrator has lent his / her personality to the story and has told the tale in a delightfully engaging manner.

Each story has an Indian sensibility – most of them are based on Indian folktales and legends and create an atmosphere that is familiar to the Indian child. Some are original stories that have been created for this series and depict urban settings that children can identify with. The purpose of this series is to encourage children to read and to transport them creatively into another world that is filled with wondrous possibility.

Will you read with us?

WILL YOU READ WITH ME?

"There is a Shiva temple on top of a hill I visit sometimes. The trees around the temple are full of monkeys. These monkeys are always eating. Over the years, I have observed that the monkeys have grown larger and fatter – in fact, some have become as huge as gorillas! Just last week on ekadasi, the poojari in the temple was commenting that it would do the monkeys good to keep the ekadasi fast also. At that time, I told him a story which my father told me when I was a little boy about how a tribe of monkeys went on a fast and what happened. Would you like to listen to the story? Will you read with me?"

Sanjay Dutt

One day, Chakrapani,
the monkey chieftain, sat on a branch of a banyan tree,
lost in his thoughts. His tribe of monkeys was
growing everyday - not because there were more
monkeys, but because the monkeys were growing fatter.

Chakku's tribe of monkeys lived near a Shiva temple
and they were always being fed all sorts of things
by people who came to visit the temple. The devotees
gave them everything - from pizza to prasād,
from curd rice to coconut.

But the monkeys' favourite food was bananas.
The thought of bananas drove
the monkeys bananas.

Pizza, pasta, nacho, noodles,
Sizzler make us drool and drool
Payāsam, pāpad, gulaab jamun,
Rossogulla are so cool, cool.

But the food that is the coolest
Is bananas, bananas, bananas...

Chakku the chieftain realised that he had a problem.
The monkeys were eating way too much,
and getting way too fat. Last week, Dinku had grown
so heavy that his favourite napping branch had snapped
under his weight. Chakku had to do something to get the
monkeys to stop eating so much.

As he sat pondering the problem, Chakku heard
the temple priest speak to the devotees.

'Tomorrow is ekādasi,' he heard the priest say,
'It is the eleventh day of the waxing moon, and on
this day, it is good to fast. Fasting cleanses the body
and the mind, and it is also a good day to spend
in meditation.'

A-ha!' thought Chakku. Here was
the solution to his problem! Chakku decided
that he would tell his monkeys that they would
have to go on a fast on ekādasi, since the humans
would be fasting on that day as well. And if
this ekādasi came often enough, maybe the
monkeys would lose a little weight.

Chakku gathered his tribe together and spoke to them. 'Tomorrow...' he began, but was interrupted by the loud chattering of two little monkeys, Bonnet and Macaque, who were fighting over a large apple. Chakku cleared his throat loudly and glared at them. They looked at him and stopped chattering.

'As I was saying,' Chakku continued,
'Tomorrow is ekādasi.'
'Eka...dosa...eka dasi...what?' Chakku was interrupted again, this time by Macaque.
'A day of one dosa' giggled Bonnet.
All the monkeys started to laugh.
'Stop it!' glared Chakku. 'On ekādasi, we have to fast for the whole day.'
'Fast?' Macaque asked not understanding.
'Eat the eka dosa really fast!' Bonnet replied laughing.
All the monkeys laughed with him.

'Bonnet and Macaque, one more sound from you, and you have had it,' Chakku threatened. 'Now as for the rest of you, a fast means not eating anything. An ekadasi fast means not eating the whole of ekadasi until the sunrise of the following day.'
There were loud gasps of shock and protest.

Chakku quickly continued, 'The humans will be
doing this, so don't we want to do it too?'
At this, the tribe calmed down and murmured
in approval. 'So, tomorrow, we will not eat
a single thing. Is that clear?' Chakku asked.

'What about breakfast?' Bonnet asked.
'No breakfast.' Chakku replied.
'Lunch?' Macaque asked.
'No! No breakfast, no lunch, no dinner!'
'But surely we can eat nuts, can't we?' Bonnet asked.
'No, you cannot eat nuts.'
'Yes, I completely agree with Chief Chakku,' an old monkey said,
'Tomorrow no eating anything except bananas.'

'NO!' Chakku said, quite exasperated now.
'No nuts, no bananas, no apples, no
guavas, no rice, no roti, nothing!
We will not eat a single thing tomorrow!'
The entire tribe was stunned into silence.
'Nothing?' asked Bonnet.
'Nothing,' replied Chakku.
'For the whole day?' asked Macaque
'Yes, for the whole day,' Chakku said, feeling
a little better that the tribe had finally understood
what he was trying to say. 'Also, we shall meditate
all day long, so that we become more calm,
peaceful and intelligent monkeys.'

.....Om Namah Shivay...!!!

.....Om Namah Shivay...!!!

......Om Namah Shivay...!!!

The next day was ekãdasi.
Chakku gathered all the other monkeys and asked
them to get ready for meditation.

With Chakku in the lead, they went
to the temple terrace.

'Om Namah Shivaya,' Chakku began seriously, closing his eyes.

'Om Namah Shivaya,' the monkeys repeated.

'Om Namah Shivaya,' Chakku chanted again

'Om Namah...'

'Chief Chakku!

Chief Chakku!' Chakku opened his eyes to see Bonnet shouting and waving his hands in the air. 'Chief Chakku, I have an idea! Instead of meditating here in the hot sun, why don't we meditate in the banana grove? The banana leaves will give us shade, and as soon as the fast is over, the bananas will be right there for us to eat.'

All the other monkeys agreed with Bonnet, and said it was a very good idea. Chakku thought about it for a while, and agreed as well. The monkeys moved to sit under the banana plants and Chakku began the meditation again.

'Om

Namah Shivaya,' he chanted.
'Om Namah Shivaya,' the monkeys repeated.
Barely had they repeated the chant a few times,
when –

'Chief Chakku! Chief Chakku!'

Without opening his eyes, Chakku recognised
Macaque's voice. 'Why don't we sit on top of
the banana plants instead of the hard ground?
That way we will be closer to heaven.'
What Macaque actually meant was that
they would be closer to the bananas!

Even though Macaque's voice was only a whisper,
all the other monkeys stopped their chanting
and had one eye open and their ears cocked
to find out what Macaque was suggesting.
They loved the idea of sitting on top of
the banana plants and meditating.
They patted Macaque's head, and commented on
what an intelligent little monkey he had become.

Chakku scratched his head. This was not how
the fast was supposed to be. But even as he was
thinking, the monkeys had dashed off to
the top of the banana plants. Chakku climbed after
them, not at all sure where all this was heading.

Just as he reached the top, Bonnet shouted,
'Chief Chakku! Chief Chakku!'

'What? What?'
Chakku snapped, very angry and irritated
by these two naughty monkeys.

'I have a better idea,' Bonnet said, 'Why don't we
pluck a banana each and hold it in our hands?
That way we can eat it as soon as the fast is over.'

This time the monkeys didn't even wait for Chakku
to respond. They all grabbed a banana each.
Bonnet thrust one in Chakku's hand too.

'Something's not right here,' Chakku thought to himself,
as he held the long banana. But still he was determined to
continue the meditation.
He started again, 'Om Namah Shivaya...'

But do you think it is possible for monkeys
to meditate with bananas in the hand?
They fidgeted and moved and no longer had
their eyes closed. Instead, they were
gazing greedily at the bananas.
Imagine their delight when they heard
Macaque's voice again:
'Chief Chakku, since we're going to be
holding the **bananas,**
why not just peel them as well?'

Before Chakku could disagree, the monkeys had
already peeled the bananas. Macaque came
to Chakku and reached for his banana.
'Let me peel it for you, Chief,' he said.
Chakku grabbed his hand away.

'Enough now! That's enough!'

Chakku shouted. 'No more distractions.
Close your eyes and meditate!'

But it was useless. The smell of all the ripe bananas
was driving the monkeys mad.
Some of the monkeys were drooling,
the others had started licking the bananas.
It was not easy for Chakku either,
but he was not ready to give in.

'Chief Chakku! Chief Chakku!'

'What is it Bonnet?' Chakku asked,
wondering what new idea the trickster was
going to come up with.
'Don't you think it would be a good idea just to
take a bite or two out of our bananas and keep it
in our mouths? As long as we don't swallow,
we will still be fasting, right?' Bonnet asked.

Chief Chakku opened his eyes to glare at Bonnet,
but found that all the monkeys had bitten off the top of the
bananas and were looking at him with their mouths *full.*

'Chief Chakku!' Macaque mumbled, his mouth full of bananas.
'Does it make a difference if we store it in our mouths or
in our stomachs? Surely, they are all part of the same body.'

'How true! How true!'

the monkeys mumbled, and swallowed the bananas quickly.

And that was how the monkeys' fast ended. Bonnet and Macaque
were hailed as heroes of the day, and a poor confused Chakku,
trying to figure out how he had been outwitted, scratched his
head, peeled his banana and ate it too.

Chakku's tribe continues to grow, and to this day, our dear chief
is still trying to find a way to make his monkeys lose weight.

I don't think he'll ever succeed. Do you?

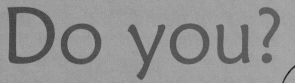

WILL YOU READ WITH ME?

WILL YOU READ WITH ME?

WILL YOU READ WITH ME?

WILL YOU READ WITH ME?